FLAT STANLEY's
WORLDWIDE ADVENTURES

BOOK No. 1

The Mount Rushmore
Calamity

The Mount Rushmore Calamity

CREATED BY **Jeff Brown**
WRITTEN BY **Sara Pennypacker**
PICTURES BY **Macky Pamintuan**

HARPER

An Imprint of HarperCollinsPublishers

Library of Congress Cataloging-in-Publication Data
Pennypacker, Sara, 1951-
    The Mount Rushmore calamity / created by Jeff Brown ; written by Sara
Pennypacker ; pictures by Macky Pamintuan. — 1st Harper Trophy ed.
    p. cm. — (Flat Stanley's worldwide adventures ; #1)
    Summary: Hoping to escape the attention brought on by the accident that
flattened Stanley, the Lambchop family drives to South Dakota, where they
become involved in a Wild West adventure at Mount Rushmore.
    ISBN 978-0-06-142991-0 (trade bdg.) — ISBN 978-0-06-142990-3 (pbk.)
    [1. Adventure and adventurers—Fiction. 2. Gold mines and mining—Fiction.
3. Vacations—Fiction. 4. Mount Rushmore National Memorial (S.D.)—Fiction.
5. South Dakota—Fiction.] I. Brown, Jeff, 1926–2003. II. Pamintuan, Macky, ill.
III. Title.
PZ7.P3856Mou 2009   2008043823
[E]—dc22   CIP
                                                                   AC

Typography by Jennifer Heuer
                    16   PC/RRD   10   9

First edition, 2009

CONTENTS

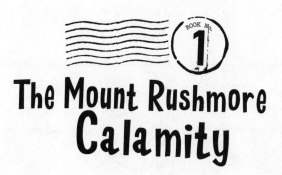

The Mount Rushmore
Calamity

Ready, Set . . .

"Sleeping bags?" George Lambchop called out to his wife, Harriet.

"Check!" answered Mrs. Lambchop.

"Wholesome snacks for the boys?"

"Check!" replied Mr. Lambchop.

The Lambchop family was preparing for their vacation to Mount Rushmore in the Black Hills of South Dakota.

They were each very excited about the adventure.

Mr. Lambchop was excited because he was going to collect another state park sticker for the rear window of the car.

Mrs. Lambchop was excited because she was going to learn more about the history of South Dakota.

Their younger son, Arthur, was excited because he was hoping to meet some real, live cowboys.

And Stanley, the Lambchops' older son, was excited because he was going somewhere nobody would recognize him.

Not long ago, Stanley had awakened

to find that his enormous bulletin board had fallen upon him during the night. Since then, the family had gotten used to having a flattened boy in the house. But when he ventured outside, he often caused a commotion: "Look, Marge! There he is . . . the famous flattened kid! Wonder what new adventure he's up to now?" Or, "Say there, Flatty, mind if we take a picture?"

The truth is, both Lambchop brothers were getting a bit tired of all the attention Stanley was getting. It would be nice, they agreed, to get away someplace where people didn't make such a fuss.

"Well, I think we're ready," said Mr.

Lambchop, surveying the mountain of suitcases and camping equipment in the hall.

"Not quite, dear," replied Mrs. Lambchop. "Remember, we still have to consult Dr. Dan about Stanley's travel needs. Better safe than sorry."

"Well, the boy is still flat," Doctor Dan pronounced, when he was finished with his examination.

"Yes, we know that," said Stanley's father. "We were wondering whether such a trip would be suitable for Stanley in his present condition. Mount Rushmore's elevation is 5,725 feet, for one thing. And we'll be traveling by automobile along the scenic highways at a fairly high velocity."

Here Mrs. Lambchop interrupted her husband with a chuckle. "Not too high a velocity, of course," she said.

Mr. Lambchop smiled at his wife's joke. Both she and Mr. Lambchop were always careful to obey local speed limits. "Still," he said, "we did feel it would be wise to check with you."

"It's a good thing you did. More people

should be concerned about the effects of travel on the body. The human being is a very complex organism. Even we doctors, with our extensive knowledge, don't completely understand it."

"Oh, dear," Mrs. Lambchop said anxiously. "Will it be all right for Stanley to come with us?"

"Of course!" said Doctor Dan. "I can't think of any reason why not!"

GO!

The next day, after a hearty breakfast, the Lambchop family began to pack the car for their big trip. In went the tent, four sleeping bags, and the rest of the camping gear. In went the suitcases, the cameras, and coolers. Arthur came out with his arms full—his authentic cowboy saddle, his authentic cowboy harmonica, and his authentic cowboy lasso.

"Oh, dear," Mrs. Lambchop murmured, surveying the overstuffed car. "There doesn't seem to be much room for the boys!"

"Playing cowboys is for little kids," Stanley said. "Now that I've been in the newspaper, I'm too grown-up for that sort of thing. I think Arthur should leave all that stuff behind."

Arthur glared at his brother. "Stanley can ride on the roof," he suggested.

Mr. Lambchop considered this. "Well, if we lash him down securely . . ."

"I think not," decided Mrs. Lambchop. "We will be pointing out many sights along the way. I don't want Stanley to miss them."

And so both boys squeezed into the backseat with much grumbling, and the family set out.

Along the way, the Lambchops did indeed come upon many wondrous sights: inspiring cityscapes, fields of bountiful crops, and numerous glories of nature.

"We should all be grateful to have good eyesight as we travel through this great land of ours," Mr. Lambchop noted. The rest of the Lambchops agreed they were very fortunate indeed.

Every time they crossed into a new state, the family recited its motto and sang its song. They played License Plate Bingo and I Spy, and the hours passed fairly quickly. Nonetheless, everyone was delighted to arrive at the gates of Mount Rushmore State Park. The boys craned their heads out the windows to gaze up at the sixty-foot-tall faces carved in the mountain, while Mr. Lambchop paid the admission fees. And as soon as the car was parked, they sprang out.

"I'm all crumpled!" Stanley groused, trying to smooth himself out.

"Well, I'm practically flattened!" complained Arthur.

"Boys, hurry along," said Mrs. Lambchop. "We're just in time to catch the last tour group."

The Lambchops fell in with a

group of cheerful-looking tourists. "In nineteen thirty-seven," the tour guide was telling them, "a bill was introduced

to add Susan B. Anthony as a fifth
face. This bill failed, so today we still
have the original four: Washington,

Jefferson, Roosevelt, and Lincoln, who is directly below us now."

Mr. and Mrs. Lambchop were fascinated by the interesting facts the tour guide related. But the boys wandered away from the group—they were still feeling a little rambunctious after spending so many hours cramped in the car.

They were also still feeling, it must be said, a little irritable with each other.

"Ha, ha!" Arthur taunted his brother from the edge of the mountain. "I can stand right out here, but you can't! You'd blow away now that you're flat!"

Suddenly, the ground shook.

"Arthur!" Stanley cried. "You'd better come ba—"

With a terrible sound, a large crack split open along Abraham Lincoln's hairline. The great carved face began to slide away down the mountainside . . . *with Arthur on it!*

Without thinking of his own safety, Stanley lunged out and grabbed hold of the retreating rock face. He held on tight. "Climb over me!" he called to his brother. "Use me as a bridge!"

Arthur did. In a moment he was back on firm ground, where Mr. and Mrs. Lambchop ran to embrace him.

Just then, a park ranger appeared.

"You! Flat Boy! Can you hold on a little longer?" he called out to Stanley. "The repair crew is on the way."

Mr. and Mrs. Lambchop were indignant. "My son has a name," Mrs. Lambchop said. "It's Stanley!"

"Sorry, ma'am," the ranger said. "I should have known better, because the same thing happens to me, too. My name is Bob, as it says right here on my name badge. But to park visitors I'm always just 'Hey, ranger!' It makes me feel very badly, indeed, as you can imagine."

Mrs. Lambchop forgave Bob, and Stanley held on until the emergency crew arrived to repair the crack. Only then did he let go. When he righted himself, he was surprised by a sea of flashing lightbulbs.

A reporter thrust a microphone in his face. "'The boy who saved Mount Rushmore'!" one reporter crowed. "That will be my headline for the evening edition!"

"'Brave boy becomes big band-aid'!" cried another.

Off to the side, Arthur crossed his arms and frowned. "Famous again," he grumbled. "And nobody knows who *I* am!"

As soon as the reporters left, Stanley

rejoined his brother in the large group that had gathered. Everyone was talking about the strange earthquake that had just happened.

"That warn't no earthquake," muttered a voice behind the boys. "That was a gold mine!"

Stanley and Arthur turned to see a girl about Stanley's age, scowling. She was wearing a worn leather vest and chaps,

and dusty boots with big silver spurs.

The boys introduced themselves.

"Good to meet you, pardners," the girl answered. "I'm the tour guide's daughter. The name's Calamity Jasper."

Calamity Jasper

The tourists dispersed, but Stanley and Arthur hung back with the cowgirl.

"What did you mean just then—about it not being an earthquake?" asked Stanley.

Calamity spread her arms out to the mountain range around them. "Thar's gold in them thar hills," she said. "Everyone knows about the gold rush of the eighteen seventies . . . rumor is there's still more in those abandoned mines. I reckon someone's dynamiting to get to it."

"Gold?" Arthur repeated. "Real gold in a real gold mine?"

"Yep," Calamity answered. "I'm about to get me some myself. I found a map."

Stanley and Arthur looked at each other. "Can we come, too?" they blurted out at the same time.

Calamity Jasper yanked her hat down and squinted at the boys. "Okeydoke," she decided at last. "I reckon you fellas could tag along. Might be needing some extra hands if I find a really big vein."

* * *

The next morning, the Lambchop family awakened in their tent to the sound of birdsong and the scent of piney woods. Everyone was eager to begin the day, but Mrs. Lambchop insisted they wait for a good breakfast.

"It's the most important meal of the day," she reminded her family. She was such a skillful cook that she made an excellent breakfast over the little campfire using only the tinned and dried provisions they had packed. The Lambchops ate with the hearty appetites brought on by outdoor living, and then they tidied the campsite. Just as the sleeping bags were being rolled up, a rustling at the tent flap caught their attention.

Calamity Jasper strode inside. "Time for all the young'uns to report to powwow!" she announced to Mr. and Mrs. Lambchop. She winked at Stanley and Arthur.

"Did you hear that, George?" exclaimed Mrs. Lambchop. "What a wonderful tour . . . so much for the boys to do!"

"Can we go?" asked Arthur and Stanley, excited.

"It's '*may* we go,' dears," Mrs. Lambchop corrected her sons. "We are not on a vacation from proper speech." Then she sent a questioning look to her husband.

"Sounds like a fine plan to me!" Mr. Lambchop said.

So the boys eagerly followed Calamity Jasper to her horse.

"This here's Gold Rush, my trusty steed," she said, patting a beautiful palomino. "Arthur, you can ride up on the saddle behind me. And you, hmm . . ." She eyed Stanley. "I'll roll you like a blanket and tie you on behind, right here under the cantle. That all right with you, buckaroo?"

"Oh, sure," Stanley said. "I am very limber." He showed her how he could bend and fold himself about, although normally he was much more modest about his abilities.

"Me, too," Arthur chimed in. "I am very limber, too." And he did a couple of somersaults in front of the cowgirl.

"Also, I am very good at holding on," Stanley said. "Remember yesterday? How I held on to Lincoln's face?"

Arthur stepped in front of his brother, holding out his lasso and his harmonica. "Also," he said, "I have a lot of

authentic cowboy gear."

"Time's a-wastin'," Calamity said, shaking her head at the boys. She rolled Stanley up, being careful to leave his head sticking out, and lashed him to the saddle. Then she stuck one boot into a stirrup and swung herself onto her horse. Last, she pulled Arthur up behind her. "Giddyap!" she called to Gold Rush, and they were off.

Trotting along the trail was very pleasant. The Lambchop boys, being from a big city, were delighted to be out in so much nature. To pass the time, Calamity taught them cowboy songs, about painful longings for home, about faithful horses, and about wide-open spaces. Things like that. The children were surprised to find that their voices were in perfect harmony, soaring and twining in the clear mountain air with astonishing beauty. Probably, in fact, no three people had ever sung cowboy songs that beautifully before. If a talent scout had happened to hear them that day, he would have signed them up to a record contract on the spot. But that's not what happened. What happened was they ran out of songs.

After that, Calamity pointed out the plants and animals along the trail. They saw pine and spruce trees and many wildflowers. They saw prairie dogs, red squirrels, deer, and even a herd of bison in the distance. "Mountain lions are native here, too," Calamity said.

"And look," said Stanley. "Mountain goats!"

"They're not native, though," Calamity Jasper told the boys. "In nineteen twenty-four, Canada gave Custer State Park six goats. They escaped their pen and began to live in the wild. There are about two hundred of them now."

Calamity was an excellent guide, and the boys were interested in all the things she told them as they rode along. But after a while, what they were really interested in was getting to the gold mine.

At last they did.

Into the Mine!

Stanley and Arthur waited impatiently while Calamity Jasper led Gold Rush to a shady spot by a stream so he could drink and munch grass. Then they followed her to the mine entrance.

Calamity handed each boy a flashlight. Then she switched on her headlamp and led them in. The mine was dark and dank. When their eyes adjusted, the boys could make out several men, blackened with dirt, chipping away at the walls and whispering to one another.

"Don't pay them any mind," Calamity whispered. "Them prospectors are a jealous bunch. Every man to himself, that kind of thing. They'll hog-tie you and throw you off the mountain if they think you're trespassing onto their claims." She nodded into the darkness. "Reckon we better mosey on a little farther."

The boys followed Calamity deeper and deeper into the dark mine shaft. The *tink-tink-tink* of the prospectors' hammers grew fainter, and the light grew dimmer.

"I don't see any gold yet!" Arthur called out to Calamity Jasper, who was far ahead now.

"Right! Where's the gold?" Stanley called out even louder.

The boys were comforted by their voices in the dark, dank mine. *"Where's the gold?"* they cried together.

"Don't yell," came Calamity's voice. "You'll cause a—"

Suddenly, there was a tremendous rumbling roar! Rocks and rubble came crashing down in front of Stanley and Arthur . . . a cave-in! So that was why everyone was whispering!

At the mine's entrance, the

prospectors dropped their hammers and ran out. "Every man for himself!" they cried. "Head for the hills!"

Stanley was tempted to call after them that they already *were* in the hills. But he was much too worried to be bothered.

"Where's Calamity

Jasper?" he asked Arthur.

The boys played their flashlights over the wall of rocks and dirt in front of them. "Do you think—" Arthur whispered.

"Shhh," Stanley whispered back.

In the quiet, the boys could make out a muffled voice: *"Gol-durned . . . gol-durned . . . gol-durned fools!"*

"Don't worry," Stanley called in—quietly—to the trapped cowgirl. "We'll get you out."

"Step aside," Arthur told his brother. "It's your fault she's in there." Then he called in to Calamity—quietly also, *"I'll* get you out. I'm very strong for my age."

Arthur *was* strong, that was true. But it was also true that he felt a lot stronger when he was wearing his Mighty Man T-shirt. And today he was wearing his authentic cowboy clothes instead.

He pushed against a big rock. He pushed and he pushed. The rock didn't budge.

"Step aside," Stanley said. "It's *your* fault she's in there. *I'll* get her out with my flatness."

Stanley surveyed the rubble in front of him. There was a gap between two big rocks about an inch wide. It might work!

He squeezed and folded himself until . . . yes! Stanley Lambchop worked himself through until he came out into a small clear space . . . and there was Calamity, sitting on a rock.

"I'm here!" he said proudly. "You can stop worrying now!"

Calamity looked up at him. "And why's that?"

"Because I'm used to being a hero. It's what I do, now that I'm flat. I rescued

my mother's favorite ring, and I helped capture sneak thieves at the Famous Museum. So I'll get you out," he assured her.

Calamity Jasper stood up and turned her head so her headlamp illuminated the small space. "Really?" she asked. "How?"

Stanley looked around. He saw the problem: *He* could get through the gap in the rocks, but *she* couldn't. "I'm sorry," he said, embarrassed. "I'll come up with something."

"Just go get help," Calamity muttered. Then she sat back down on the rock and turned her back to him.

Stanley worked himself back through

to the other side.

"My flatness didn't help," he admitted to Arthur.

"Well, my strength didn't help either," Arthur said. "Too bad we couldn't combine the two—hey!" He jumped up. "We've been studying machines at school! Do you know how a lever works?"

Stanley understood Arthur's clever idea at once. The boys rolled a small rock beside the larger one, and Stanley lay himself over it. He worked his feet under the large rock and made himself stiff as a board. "Use your strength to press down on my shoulders," he directed his brother.

Arthur did. With a deep creak, the boulder rolled aside!

Calamity Jasper crawled through the gap. She narrowed her eyes and scowled at the two boys as she stormed past them to the mine entrance.

The boys followed, and after the three children rubbed their eyes in the bright afternoon sunshine, they stared in disbelief: Gold Rush was gone!

On the Trail

"Must-a been spooked by the cave-in," Calamity moaned. "I'll have to track him before he gets too far!"

The boys kept a safe distance behind—Calamity didn't seem in any mood for their company. Now and then they heard her muttering, "Gol-durned show-offs!" and they dropped back even farther.

Stanley and Arthur felt miserable. They *had* been show-offs, and they knew it now.

After a while, Calamity gave a little whoop and ran into a clearing. There stood Gold Rush, snorting and lathered in sweat. The cowgirl threw her arms around her horse. "Let's get you some water, fella," she said.

Calamity looked around. "We're a ways off from the stream," she worried out loud. "And I don't see any signs of a spring . . ."

"I can help! I have an idea!" Stanley cried.

Calamity shot him a look that said

she'd heard just about enough from him. But Stanley did indeed have an idea.

He lay down in the grass in front of Gold Rush and curved himself into the shape of a trough. "Pour in some water from the canteens," he directed Calamity.

Calamity did, and then Stanley held very still as the horse's big lips came right down and slurped from his belly. It tickled, but

Stanley Lambchop did not move. And he did not spill one drop.

When Gold Rush had finished drinking, Calamity helped Stanley to his feet. She wore a big grin as she shook his hand. "Maybe I was wrong about you, pardner," she said. "Any friend of my horse is a friend of mine."

"So you're not angry with us anymore?" asked Arthur.

"Shucks, no. I reckon you two aren't half bad for a couple of greenhorns. Now I better fix us some grub. We're lost, pardners. We're gonna have to figure out how we get home from here. A cowboy can't think on an empty stomach."

Calamity Jasper pulled a can of beans and a pot from her saddlebags. She built a fire, and soon the beans were bubbling cheerfully in the pot. "Cowboys always carry beans for emergencies," she confided.

Arthur made a mental note to carry beans with him from now on. "How did you learn to be a cowboy?" he asked Calamity. "How did you learn to follow tracks like that? We didn't see anything, but you followed right to Gold Rush."

"Following tracks isn't a cowboy skill. I'm part Lakota Sioux," Calamity said proudly. "We Native Americans know lots of useful things, like which plants make medicine and how to hunt and fish and how to use— Whoa, doggie! *Smoke signals!*"

Calamity jumped to her feet. She ordered Arthur to gather a load of tumbleweeds. When he returned, she piled the tumbleweeds onto the camp-fire. Immediately, a dark thick smoke streamed upward.

"What about a blanket?" Stanley asked. "Don't you need a blanket for smoke signals?"

Calamity grinned. "That's where you come in, pardner!"

Both boys understood at once. Arthur picked up Stanley's feet, and Calamity took hold of his arms. Together, they flapped Stanley over the fire, sending

puffs of thick smoke into the clear air. Stanley very bravely held his breath and didn't cough once.

Before too long, they heard a rustling in the bushes at the edge of the clearing. The tour group!

"We saw the signals," Calamity's father said. "Came to see what you youngsters were up to."

"Looks like they're up to a real Wild West time!" said George Lambchop. "What a trip, eh, boys?"

Around the Campfire

The children were grateful to follow the tour group back along the trail. As they crested Mount Rushmore over Lincoln's face, the boys walked to the edge to take a look. The repair crew had done an excellent job. The crack was barely visible.

Stanley stepped out even farther. "See, Arthur," he boasted. "See, I can

too stand out here!"

But just then a sudden gust of wind caught Stanley by surprise. It swept him off his feet, and he went skittering down Lincoln's steep forehead, coming to rest on the bridge of Lincoln's long nose!

Stanley held on for dear life. He looked around . . . far, far above him he saw Arthur, looking terribly worried. And suddenly he was very glad his brother had brought his authentic cowboy gear with him . . .

"Arthur!" he cried. "Throw down your lasso!"

Arthur uncoiled his lasso and swung it around and around, aiming. Then he let go, and the rope went sailing out into the South Dakota sky . . . and landed right in front of Stanley's outstretched hand!

Calamity Jasper gave Arthur an admiring nod. "Mighty fine twirling, buckaroo!" she applauded. "Mighty fine."

Stanley grabbed hold of the rope and tied it around his waist. "Bring me up, Arthur!" he called.

Just then, another gust of wind blew across the mountain. It lifted Stanley Lambchop up like a kite, up and up until the lasso was stretched taut. Stanley flew high above the tour group!

"Boys!" Mrs. Lambchop called, when

she saw what was going on. "Quit that horsing around!"

"Now dear, the boys are just having a bit of fun," Mr. Lambchop said. "It's their vacation, too,

after all. I don't see the harm."

"I suppose you're right, George," Mrs. Lambchop said. "Still, I noticed Stanley smelled strongly of smoke, and that is not good for a growing boy. I'd like him to come back to camp and change his clothes. Arthur, reel your brother in now, please."

When Stanley was back on earth, Mr. Lambchop invited Calamity to join them for a cookout. After a delicious meal of hot dogs and hamburgers, Mrs. Lambchop said, "I believe this celebration calls for s'mores!" to cheers all around.

While they were toasting the marshmallows, Stanley and Arthur apologized for causing so much trouble in the mine earlier. "Also, we're sorry you didn't find any gold," Arthur said. "You have nothing to show for all that time in the mine."

"Well, that ain't exactly so, pardner," Calamity said with a grin. She dug into her pocket and produced a large gleaming gold nugget. "I found it in my boot. Reckon it fell in during the cave-in."

"Real gold!" breathed Arthur. "Can I hold it?"

"You can do more than hold it, pardner," Calamity said with a mysterious smile. "You got a hammer?"

Arthur fetched the hammer they

had packed to pound in the tent stakes. Calamity placed the nugget on a flat rock and brought the hammer down hard, cracking it into three chunks of gold. She gave one to Stanley and one to Arthur. "They're yours, you earned them," she said to the brothers. "Way I

see it, without the cave-in, I wouldn't have had the gold in the first place. And without you, there wouldn't have been no cave-in."

And with that, Calamity Jasper mounted her trusty steed, waved good-bye, and rode off into the sunset.

There's No Place
Like Home

The next day was the last of their
vacation. Calamity was off at a rodeo,
and the Lambchops were enjoying the
park as a family. Many interesting
activities filled the day, but Mr. and
Mrs. Lambchop noticed the boys
seemed subdued.

"It's the lack of fresh vegetables and

fruits, George," Mrs. Lambchop fretted back at the campsite that afternoon.

"I dare say you're right, dear," Mr. Lambchop said. "You know the boys so well."

Just as they were packing up, a park ranger strode into their camp.

"Why, hello there, Bob," Mrs. Lambchop greeted him, remembering how he felt about his name.

"Hello, Lambchops all," Ranger Bob said. "Sure are sorry to see you folks go."

"We've had a grand time," Mr. Lambchop told him. "Worth every penny of our admission fees!"

"That's what I'm here about," said

Ranger Bob. "Your brave son Stanley paid his fee like everyone else, and given what a hero he was, something doesn't seem right about that. I'm here to refund that fee, with the park's gratitude!"

"Excuse me," Stanley interrupted politely, "but my brother was a hero, too. If it weren't for him being out there, I would never have grabbed on to the face of that rock."

"I can see how that is," agreed the ranger. "Two heroes, two refunds it is!"

Then Ranger Bob personally affixed the Mount Rushmore State Park sticker to the rear window of the Lambchops' car, and bade them a safe trip home.

Mrs. Lambchop looked into the car, overstuffed once more. "I'm sorry, boys, but . . ."

"No," said Stanley. "Arthur can have the space. You can mail me home. I don't mind."

So the Lambchops drove to the nearest post office and slipped their elder son into a large mailing envelope, along with the rest of the graham crackers, a slice of American cheese, and a deck of cards.

"Insurance?" asked the postmaster.

Mr. Lambchop chuckled as if the postmaster had made a good joke. "No need. There's no finer postal system in the world. I say, if you can't trust the United States Postal Service to deliver a package safely, then whom can you trust?"

Mrs. Lambchop asked that the envelope be marked Fragile, but Stanley was horrified at that suggestion. He did

allow the postmaster to stamp Do Not Bend, however.

And then the four Lambchops made their way home from South Dakota: three of them in a car, and one in postal trucks and planes.

* * *

Stanley arrived home first, refreshed by his restful trip, and helped unpack the car when his weary family appeared.

"It's always good to get away," Mr. Lambchop noted with a sigh. "But . . ."

"But it's always good to get back home," finished his wife.

Then Stanley and Arthur hurried to their room to unpack, while their parents tended to the stack of mail that had piled up.

Arthur pinned the newspaper article about them up on the bulletin board. "BROTHER HEROES!" read the headline above a photo of the boys smiling with their arms around each

other. "You know, Stanley," he said, "I don't think I ever thanked you for what you did—becoming a bridge for me to cross over."

"Well, I didn't thank you either, for lassoing me when I fell down the mountain," Stanley replied. He unpacked the two gold nuggets and placed them on the bookcase. "Brotherhood is more important than gold!"

"Right!" agreed Arthur. "And it's more important than any girl, too! Even a cowgirl!"

"Right," said Stanley. "Brothers above all!"

"Boys, there's a postcard here," Mrs. Lambchop's voice interrupted them.

"It's from Calamity Jasper."

"For me!" Stanley and Arthur each cried at the same time.

"It's addressed to Cowpoke Lamb-chop," their mother called out. "I'll leave it here in the hall."

In their haste to see whom it was for, Stanley and Arthur, the brothers above all, nearly trampled each other running out of their room.

The End

WHAT YOU NEED TO KNOW TO BE A BLACK HILLS GOLD MINER

Native Americans have lived in the Black Hills for more than 9,000 years. Some Lakota believe the Black Hills are the sacred center of the world.

The Black Hills Gold Rush began in 1874, when Colonel Custer led a thousand men into the western part of South Dakota to investigate reports that the area contained gold. That's the same Custer who later had his Last Stand against Sitting Bull at the Battle of Little Big Horn.

One of the most famous cowgirls of the Black Hills was named Calamity Jane. She was a good friend of the famous lawman Wild Bill Hickock.

Gold was first discovered in the Black Hills just a few miles from where Mount Rushmore was later built.

Some would-be miners get tricked by "fool's gold," which looks a lot like the real thing. If you want to tell the difference, try pressing your fingernail into the surface. If it leaves a small indent, you've found gold!

The heads on Mount Rushmore are as tall as a six-story building. If you matched them with bodies, the men with those heads would be three times as tall as the Statue of Liberty!

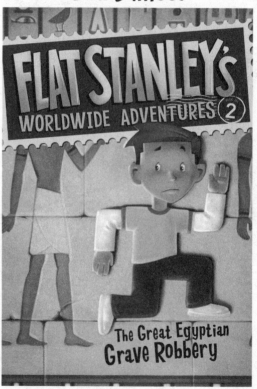

A Letter for Stanley

George Lambchop was sitting at the kitchen table, going through the mail as his wife cooked breakfast. "Look at these beauties, Harriet!" he called, holding up a letter with many exotic stamps in the corner. "From Egypt!"

Ever since their eldest son, Stanley, had been flattened by a bulletin board and could now travel by mail, the Lambchop family had become keenly interested in stamps.

"In a minute, dear," Mrs. Lambchop said. "I'm just at the difficult part of flipping this French toast. A letter from Egypt, you say! Why don't you open it and read it to me."

Mr. Lambchop began to do just that, but then he caught himself. "That was a close one!" he cried. "It's a federal offense to open mail that's addressed to someone else. This letter is for Stanley!"

Just then, both Lambchop boys appeared in the doorway, drawn by the delicious aroma of French toast and bacon.

"Stanley, son, letter for you here. Looks important."

"What about me?" Stanley's younger brother, Arthur, asked. "Any mail for me today?"

"Not today, sorry," Mr. Lambchop replied. "But, Stanley, why don't you open yours and read it to us over breakfast."

"*After* breakfast," Mrs. Lambchop said firmly. "*And* hand washing. You know how maple syrup gets all over everything."

The boys finished their breakfast

and washed up. Then Stanley opened his letter.

"If you are the world-famous flattened boy of America," he read out loud, "and if you are less than three inches thick, you must come to Egypt at once. We are beginning an archaeological project and are in urgent need of someone of your dimensions."

"I don't know about *world-famous*," Arthur grumbled—a bit enviously, it must be said.

"Maybe they've got the wrong person."

"But I *am* only half an inch thick." Stanley sighed. "So that's me, all right."

"*I,*" Mrs. Lambchop corrected her son. "That is *I.*"

"It's signed Sir Abu Shenti Hawara the fourth," Stanley said, "and look: He's taken care of my travel arrangements." Stanley held up a very large envelope covered with stamps.

George Lambchop took the letter and read it over. "No mention of Stanley's *family* going with him," he said, frowning. "I don't know . . ."

"Well, an archaeological project . . . it's not as if it's something dangerous.

And travel *is* broadening, George . . . ,"
Mrs. Lambchop mused. "Oh, Stanley,
darling . . . I didn't mean it that way!
What I meant was, it rounds out one's
education . . . oh my, that didn't come
out quite right either!"

"Well, your mother and I have
always encouraged you boys to lend
a helping hand when needed," Mr.
Lambchop said. "I suppose that goes
even if it's needed halfway around the
world."

"We'd better take you to the post
office at once, Stanley," Mrs. Lambchop
said. "I will pack the leftover French
toast and bacon for you to eat on the
way. No maple syrup, of course. It

wouldn't do to arrive all sticky!"

"Something to drink?" Stanley asked.

"I think not, dear," his mother told him. "Egypt is quite a distance, and I'm afraid you won't be near a bathroom for some time. Which reminds me . . ." And she went off to pack a toothbrush and washcloth for her son's trip.

Stanley noticed that Arthur seemed glum. He knew Arthur sometimes found it difficult being the only round brother in a family. "Would you like me to bring back something from Egypt for you?" he asked.

"Hmmmph," Arthur replied. "If you're going to Egypt, you should bring me back a mummy."

"I don't believe they offer those as souvenirs. And besides, it wouldn't fit in the envelope with Stanley!" chuckled the boys' father. Mr. Lambchop was known for his sharp sense of humor. "How about a nice postcard?" Mr. Lambchop was known for being a practical thinker, too.

Arthur folded his hands across his chest. "A mummy or nothing."

Stanley was very sorry to see his brother looking so grumpy as he slid himself into the envelope.

***

Read THE GREAT EGYPTIAN GRAVE ROBBERY
and all of Flat Stanley's Worldwide Adventures!
To find out more, go to www.flatstanleybooks.com.